My Pretty Ballerina ®

In the Spotlight

By Karen Backstein • Illustrated by Cathy Beylon

SCHOLASTIC INC.

New York   Toronto   London   Auckland   Sydney

To my niece, Jessica, the
prettiest one of them all

ISBN 0-590-45144-8
Copyright © 1991 Tyco Industries, Inc.
My Pretty Ballerina trademark
and likeness used under license from Tyco Industries, Inc.
All rights reserved.
12 11 10 9 8 7 6 5 4 3 2 1   1 2 3 4 5 6/9
Printed in the U.S.A.   2 4
First Scholastic printing, September 1991

I think being a ballerina is the most wonderful
thing in the world.

Especially when I'm on stage dancing.
That makes me happy!
Bright pink and blue spotlights shine on me, and I
feel so pretty in my fluffy tutu.

Guess what?
Our class recital is next week, and I get to dance
a solo!
That means I will be all alone on the stage.
Everyone in the class is *very* excited about
the show.
We're all practicing hard.

Oops! Maybe we have to practice harder.

Our teacher, Miss Marie, says we need *lots* of work
if we want to become beautiful, graceful ballerinas.

Over and over, we point our toes and bend low
until we touch the ground.
Miss Marie calls out the steps.
"On your toes, *relevé! Assemblé! Tendu! Plié!*"
We're getting better all the time!

But we're not perfect yet!

"Remember, we have our first dress rehearsal
tomorrow night," Miss Marie announces.
"We will dance the whole ballet."

All night I dream of spotlights. All day I long
for rehearsal.
I can't wait to dance!

I'm usually the first dancer to arrive at our
ballet studio, but tonight everyone is early.
Tutus and shiny pink slippers with satin ribbons
fill the room.
"Look at me!" my best friend Jordan squeals.
It's her first recital, and her first tutu.

Jordan and I run onto the stage.
Something is wrong!
It's dark and creepy, and Miss Marie isn't here.
Finally, Miss Greyson arrives.
Miss Greyson plays piano for our class.

"Girls," she says quietly. "Miss Marie just
telephoned. She has the flu!
We'll have to cancel the recital!"

Cancel the recital? That would mean no
spotlights! No solo!
I can't let that happen!

"Miss Greyson," I beg, "Miss Marie already taught us all the steps. Can't we try to put on the show ourselves?" Miss Greyson agrees. "But who will be the director?" "You can do it!" Jordan says to me. "I know you can. You taught me all those steps when I first came to ballet class." "All right. Take your places!" I call. Miss Greyson begins to play. The dancers begin to dance.

Oh, no! *Everything's* going wrong!

I feel terrible—like hundreds of butterflies are dancing in my stomach. I even forget my own steps!
It's not easy being a leader.

Maybe we should just give up.
But then I look at Jordan. She's so disappointed!
"I never danced on stage before," she says
tearfully, "and now I never will!"

"Let's try again," I say.
Everyone cheers!

I remember what Miss Marie did, and I call out the steps.
Then we dance again.

This time, I remember all my steps.

When we finish, Miss Greyson applauds.
"That was wonderful!"

Every night that week we rehearse.
We work harder than we ever have before.
After all, we want Miss Marie to be proud of us.

Finally, the night of the recital has arrived.
Look at us! We soar, we spin, we flutter
and float.

Best of all, Miss Marie is in the audience!
When I dance my solo, she applauds and shouts,
"Encore, My Pretty Ballerina!"
That's what you say when you want the ballerina to
dance again.

And I do—because being a ballerina is the best thing in the world.

Relevé (REH-le-vay)

Assemblé (Ah-SAHM-blay)

Tendu (TAHN-doo)

Plié (PLEE-ay)